Born in Staffordshire and spending some time growing up in West Yorkshire, the author had a very varied and interesting childhood. He had always had a keen interest in theatre and film and on leaving school worked for Moss Empires then went on to work for The J Arthur Rank Organization. He is a very enthusiastic and passionate historian and a dedicated Richardian of many years standing.

Harry J Tomkinson

TREACHERY AT BOSWORTH FIELD, 1485

AUSTIN MACAULEY PUBLISHERS™
LONDON • CAMBRIDGE • NEW YORK • SHARJAH

A CIP catalogue record for this title is available from the British Library.

ISBN 9781786938138 (Paperback)
ISBN 9781786938145 (E-Book)
www.austinmacauley.com

First Published (2017)
Austin Macauley Publishers Ltd.
25 Canada Square
Canary Wharf
London
E14 5LQ

Dedication

This work is dedicated to the memory of my dear late wife, Ann, who has always supported me in everything that I have undertaken.

Preface

Being somewhat of an amateur historian, I have always been interested in Richard III.

And how it seemed to me that history has dealt him a cruel blow over very many years. Of course the Tudor propaganda machine kicked in immediately after the battle of Bosworth. But it seemed to me that it was more than just that. He was held up as the ultimate figure of an evil wicked uncle, a tyrant, a murderer, a man who wanted to grab the throne for himself. And rule with supreme authority. As in William Shakespeare's version in his famous play, Richard III. The more I started to look at King Richard III and his life, the more convinced I became that he was none of these, ether as King or man. And in fact, I think that we may have to thank William Shakespeare for his version of this play. Because for good or bad, what it has done over all these years, is to fire people's interest in King Richard III, all over the world.

Otherwise Richard may have become just another English King, that no one was particularly bothered about finding. Interest was no more apparent than when the remains of King Richard III, were found in a council car park in Leicester back in 2012. Media from all over the world descended on Leicester. And the re-internment of King Richard in 2015, where crowds lined the footpaths and in some places were twelve deep. This interest goes on and on, you only have to walk into any bookshop or go on line to be overwhelmed by the enormity of the subject. In some cases the malignant of Richard still goes on even today, as certain documentaries and performances try to ridicule and discredit him. We know that Henry Tudor tried his very best to discredit Richard in any way that he could, but maybe now, just maybe, the wheel of fortune starts to turn once again.

In writing this novel I have tried to portray what may have happened, during these times of Richard's life. A sort of snapshot in time. In researching some of the material for this book, I was astounded by how many strong characters there are in this period of the so-called 'War of the Roses' in particular the roles of the many women, which I could not help but have immense admiration for. Women like Anne Neville, Margaret Beaufort, Margaret of Anjou, Cicely Neville, Elizabeth Woodville and many more. I have also written it as maybe King Richard would have wrote it, if he had lived to tell the tale. Not wishing to add or detract from the known facts. This is my own fictional story as I see it. Or Perhaps Richard III last Plantagenet King of England may have seen it.

It is my hope that you may enjoy reading this and perhaps give one of our great Kings of England Richard III, a chance to put the records straight. A chance that he never had in his very short life and reign.

Ode for King Richard III

O Richard my King, most noble and gallant knight.

How long have you been abandoned and left in this place amongst the cold dark earth, with not even a clout to cover you.

The years are very many, some five hundred and twenty seven in all.

But it seems just yesterday, that we were forming up outside the White Boar Inn in Leicester to ride out and destroy that Welsh rebel, who for many years had hidden himself away, across the waters in Brittany and France. That vile pretender of the Beaufort's womb, whose Grandfather Owen did seduce King Henry's Queen. This was the man that some called Henry Tudor.

My Lord, you were ever the brave and loyal knight that took up arms for England and St. George against this Tudor, who refused to fight, and instead skulked away down at the edge of the battlefield awaiting the Stanley treachery that was to come.

In all your life your rulings were fair and as a King your laws were just. O my Richard, my King and liege Lord, if God had granted you a little more time how different may things have been, but it was not to be, Your beloved son, Edward Prince of Wales, was taken from you, and then your soul mate, your wife and childhood sweetheart Anne Neville. How lonely you became Richard as you felt the treachery cutting into you on Redemore Field, I wonder if your last thoughts were of them.

The Greyfriars cared for you and watched over you, even though Henry's men gave them little time to bury you and certainly not with honour and dignity. The humble friars would come each day to pray for you. Until the day came when the Tudor's son, now King Henry VIII, had your last abode reduced to rubble and flattened.

Richard, you were gone forever or so we thought!

But wait, my Lord, here you are, we have found you at last, you are not lost but saved. You have been re-interred in great splendour, as a King of England should be, with all honour and dignity. Your funeral cask was lovingly made by your 17th great nephew, from English oak hewn from an ancient forest. And now we see slowly, the great injustice that was heaped on you in death is being reversed.

Thank God for Richard III Plantagenet King of England, France and Lord of Ireland 1452-1485.

"May he rest in peace and rise in glory."

The Main Characters of This Story

House of York
Plantagenet

Richard III King of England, France and Lord of Ireland

Edward of Middleham: Prince of Wales (Ned)

Katherine Plantagenet: (Kate)

John Plantagenet: (Johnny)

John de la Pole: Earl of Lincoln (Richards Nephew)

(Proclaimed Richards heir to the Throne – Jack)

House of Lancaster Tudor

Henry Tudor: Henry VII
Margaret Beaufort: Countess of Richmond
Jasper Tudor: Duke of Bedford Earl of Pembroke
(Henry Tudor's Uncle)

House of Lancaster

Margaret of Anjou: Queen consort of England
Edward of Westminster: Prince of Wales

House of Neville

Richard Neville: Earl of Warwick (Kingmaker)
Anne Beauchamp: Countess of Warwick; His Wife
Isabel Neville: Warwick's elder Daughter
To Marry: George Duke of Clarence Plantagenet
Anne Neville: Warwick's younger Daughter
To marry 1st. Edward of Westminster
2nd. Richard III King Of England
Queen Consort to Richard III of England

House of Woodville

Elizabeth Woodville: Queen Consort to Edward IV
Elizabeth Woodville: Edward IV daughter
King Richard's niece (Bess)

Viscount Francis Lovell
King Richard's most faithful and loyal friend
John Howard Duke of Norfolk a loyal friend

John de Vere Earl of Oxford: Henry Tudor's
Main commander in the field

Participants at Bosworth

List of the main participants in each of the armies
that were engaged in the battle of Bosworth Field

King Richard's Army:

John Howard: Duke of Norfolk
Francis Lovell: Viscount
The Earl of Surrey (Norfolk's son)
Sir Richard Ratcliffe
Sir Humphrey Stafford
Sir Robert Brackenbury
Sir Robert Percy
Sir William Conyers
Sir William Catesby
Sir Percival Thirlwall
Walter Devereux: Lord Ferrers of Chartley

Henry Percy: Earl of Northumberland
(Did not take part in the battle)
Thomas Lord Stanley
(Committed to Henry Tudor) Sir William Stanley
(Committed to Henry Tudor)

Henry Tudor's Army:

John de Vere: Earl of Oxford
Jasper Tudor: Earl of Pembroke
Sir Gilbert Talbot
Sir Rhys ap Thomas

Sir John Savage
Sir John Cheyney
Sir William Brandon
Lord Sir Thomas Stanley
Sir William Stanley

Substantial Welsh contingents
French Mercenaries
Scottish Mercenaries

Prologue

The battle of Bosworth Field took place on the 22nd of August 1485, which is near to the village of Sutton Cheney, Leicestershire.

It is approximately thirteen miles from Leicester, (travelling by today's roads) and quite near to the old Roman road of Watling Street.

Richard III had been on the throne for just over two years, after the death of his brother Edward IV. He had faced many challenges in that time. The Woodvilles' vying for power, and the illegitimacy of his brothers' children. Not the least of these being the acquisition of treachery by Lord Hastings and then The Buckingham Rebellion of 1483. Added to all of this was also the under lying threat of invasion by the Henry Tudor faction in France and Brittany. Which was being fuelled by his mother, Margaret Beaufort, Countess of Richmond and Lord Thomas Stanley's wife.

Henry Tudor landed at Mill Bay, near to Milford Haven South Wales, on the 7th August 1485 with his army and proceeded to make his way up and across to Shrewsbury. Eventually hoping to make his way to London and picking up supporters on the way. King Richard had suspected the invasion at some point and had moved his court from London, to Nottingham

Castle. To be nearer to the Centre of the country, so that he could effectively strike at an invasion from wherever it may occur.

When King Richard's spies reported back that the Tudor army had landed in Mill Bay, Richard made his way to Leicester and then to make camp at Sutton Cheney. Where he hoped to intercept Henry Tudor, close by and prevent him from reaching London.

Chapter One
Nottingham Castle
April 1484

Nottingham Castle looks down and dominates the town of Nottingham.

Perched as it is on the top of a steep sandstone cliff, skirted below by the River Leen. It is a huge vast fortress and seems almost to reach the sky at times.

It had for centuries been the royal castle and residence in the midlands. It was one of the most secure castles offering three separate baileys, each of these had a deep moat. Eight years before, Edward IV had refurbished the castle to a very high standard. And had constructed spacious royal apartments, which provided much comfort. When Richard became King he also undertook restoration work here. This was one of Richard's favourite places outside of Yorkshire. He called it his "Castle of Care". It was where he felt he could relax with Anne and go hunting in the beautiful Bestwood Park or even in Sherwood itself. Richard and Anne had been here for some weeks, having made their way up from London and were to go on eventually to his castle in Middleham to see their dear son Edward. They had to leave him at Middleham in the charge of

Anne Idley his governess and Isabel Burgh his nurse, who doted on the lad.

Edward these days seemed to be always in a state of not being too well and unable to travel very far. Certainly not by horseback, Richard had to arrange for a litter to transport him to his investiture as Prince of Wales in September 1483 in York. Amide tremendous celebrations which lasted for three weeks in August and September. The people of York do love him so.

Richard had lain awake most of the night not wanting to disturb Anne.

They had always slept together in the same bed since their marriage twelve years ago. It was such a comfort to know that Anne was there for him, he loved her so very much. His beautiful Anne, she was always so understanding.

When Richard 16th Earl of Warwick had married Anne off to Edward of Westminster, to cement the union with Margaret of Anjou against his brother Edward IV it had broken Richard's heart. Richard had always been in love with Anne, from his very early childhood days in Yorkshire living in the Neville family home at Middleham. Anne would tease him and bait him, but always would be seen near to him. Even in the tilt yard, where Richard, Francis Lovell and sometimes Rob Percy would practice their sword play. Many were the times when Anne would long to take up a sword and spar with her Dickon. She would pull Francis to one side and beg him to take messages to her Dickon. Then it was

Richard's turn to tease her. She would go off and sulk, but always return to watch him. She would beg her father to let her go out hunting with Richard and Francis.

Anne's older sister by four years, Isabel, was sometimes jealous of Anne and her friendship with these boys, as she would call them, and would go see her mother to report on Anne's behaviour. Which did not go down well with Anne, as the Countess would then take her to task for not having a chaperone and following a lady like protocol, even though she was still only a child.

Richard, Francis and Anne were inseparable, they could be found almost everywhere together. And even on days when they were not allowed out of the castle, they were to be found harassing the kitchen staff, or running riot around the battlements. But when Anne had to do her embroidery with my lady Anne her mother and Isabel, the castle was strangely still. So at these times Richard and Francis, if not in the tilt yard, would be at their studies. At dinner Anne would be furious if anyone but Francis sat alongside of Richard, but she would always sit on his other side. Despite Isabel pointing out to her mother and father that Anne should be on the top table with them. The Earl would smile and her mother would look disapprovingly at her. Isabel and Anne did not very often get on together as sisters. Isabel being the elder, tried to always put Anne in her place. But Anne, as soon as Isabel's back was turned would make faces at her sister. In bed at night Isabel would tell Anne that their father the Earl, had promised to make sure that she would marry well and one day would be a princess and maybe even a Queen. Anne would retort with, well I care not. I will marry Dickon and be his Queen. Then a fight would break out and always end with Anne in tears. Their mother Lady Anne Beauchamp 16th Countess of Warwick was a very strong minded lady and came from a noble and old English/ Norman family. Lady Anne would have to spend long periods of time, running the household and attending to the day to day matters that needed to be seen to, in running and maintaining such a large and important castle such as Middleham. Because her husband the Earl of Warwick, was very often away on court matters and the Kings business.

Of course the Earls steward, would have seen to most things, but it still fell on Lady Anne to make decisions in the absence of her husband and also to ensure that the other residences in the area, which the Earl owned where being looked after. Such as Sherriff Hutton and Barnard's Castle. Nevertheless Lady Anne would try to find time not only for her daughters, but for her other guests. Such as young Richard and Francis, who were there really to be brought up as gentlemen. To be educated and learn the many skills needed to become chivalrous knights. The Earl Richard Neville, acted as guardian to the boys on the orders of Edward IV. Afternoons would usually find Lady Anne with her ladies and two daughters in her solar, talking and embroidering. Richard and Francis at this time would be with their tutor. Ether learning Latin or French and studying geography and history. But also learning about how to control finances. And not forgetting how to behave at court and good manners. Richard and Francis, like most boys of their age, would have much preferred to be out riding and hunting in the dales. Or having lessons in the tilt yard. All of this was running through Richard's thoughts as lay there half awake and half asleep. The times they had when they were all young at

Middleham, The hunting trips out from the castle, when the Earl with his guests would lead out in front, trotting over the bridge. And then they broke into a cantor, then gallop. Out across the dales. The falconers' having a job to try and keep up, with the birds to take care of. Sometimes on these occasions we were allowed to take part also, even Ann and Isabel along with the Countess and her ladies would ride out. Anne was always to be seen galloping in between Francis and me, her long hair streaming out behind her. Isabel quite a way back, with the Lady Anne and the ladies. O what days they were. O what happy glorious days. Aare we could return again to those days, maybe when Ned is well.

We three and Francis will once more scatter the sheep as we gallop across the dales. Though I fear it may not be for some time yet.

Francis is my best and most loyal friend in all the world. Although he is two years my younger, we are like twin brothers. He became a ward of my brother Edward IV after Lord Lovell died in 1465. I remember how we were not the only boys being educated at Middleham around this time. But somehow Francis and I became inseparable and just seemed to share much of the same values. We had the same sense of humour and some of the other lads just could not see what we found so funny at times. Looking back now, these were very happy times and just went by us so quickly that we hardly noticed. I think also sometimes that Anne could be quite jealous of Francis, as we spent so much time together. And she hated being told to go and play with her dolls. But at other times she used Francis as a go between. And would sometimes try and make me jealous of Francis by flirting with him. Even leading him by the arm and whispering in his ear, then turning to see if I was looking. Francis, of course, knew how to play Anne's little games and would wink at me out of the corner of his eye.

Richard could not sleep, with so many things weighing heavy on his mind. In the end he decided to rise as quietly as he could, so as not to disturb Anne. It was still the early hours. As he moved from their bed he caught sight of Anne, her beautiful face, so innocent in sleep and then she stirred just slightly, Richard, what is it, is something wrong. It is nothing my sweet, the hour is yet early, sleep on awhile and worry not. Richard put on his robe and made his way outside the royal bedroom, His guards immediately sprang to their feet, Richard motioned to them that all was well. Richard's bedroom guards were well used to him moving about the castle in the small hours, so this was no surprise to them. He made his way down the back staircase that lead to one of the four chapels in the castle, this one because of its location to the royal apartments was used as a private chapel. He often came here when he needed to be alone, think and pray. It was cold, there was a chill in the air, but he did not mind that. He knelt in front of the altar and prayed for Anne and then for young Ned, that the Lord would heal him and make him well again. O, he so wanted him to be well, to be able to take up his duties as Prince of Wales and to learn about his people and their needs. To learn how to be a good and just governor. All of these things Richard had instilled in the lad and he knew that Edward perhaps one day, the Lord be willing. Would be a great and glorious King, in hopefully a kingdom of England that would be united and peaceful once again. Richard prayed for his mother Cecily Dowager Duchess of York. She was back now living at Berkhamstead. Cecily, The strong willed lady of the of the York family, who had to endure so very many things throughout her life. Richards mind flew back to when he was just seven years old, after the battle of Wakefield his father, the Duke of York had been mercilessly killed and his brother Edmund had been murdered trying to escape from Sandal Castle.

His mother had stood steadfast throughout this most difficult time, she was a pillar of strength and held the family together, as she had always done. She had born thirteen children, with only seven surviving into childhood. Much like Richards love for Anne, his mother and father were also very much in love and their marriage had been a complete love match, and one of mutual respect for one another.

His brother Edward came to mind, his good brother Edward IV, the first Yorkist King, who had ruled England for some twenty one years, until his sudden illness and death. The affection that he had for his brother, the trust that Edward had placed in him, knowing that Richard would be loyal and carry out whatever he asked of him. Of the power struggles that went on within Edward's court. In particular because of the favours that Edward bestowed on his in-laws, the Woodville/Grey/Rivers side of his new family at court.

It was a complete surprise, I think to all of us, when Edward announced his marriage to Elizabeth Woodville. None more so than Richard Earl of Warwick, who had been instrumental in bringing him to the throne. And was also planning for Edward to marry a French Princess, Bona of Savoy. This would have created an alliance between the two counties. The Earl was totally against this marriage to Elizabeth, as he could foresee the damage that it would cause at court. Edward would have none of it, he was totally besotted with Elizabeth. I must say that she was a most beautiful and enchanting lady and Edward always did have an eye for beautiful women.

There were days when you could almost cut the atmosphere at court, but Edward seemed to be most oblivious to what was happening. He would publicly shun and humiliate Warwick in favour of his in-laws. The problems at court refused to go away, with the Woodville's becoming yet more powerful. So much so, that in the end Warwick just stormed out of court, he could not stand it anymore. This could and very nearly was, the downfall of the house of York, but still Edward buried his head in the sand. We heard of plots by Warwick to oust Edward and eventually, my other brother George, head strong Duke of Clarence, left court and threw in his lot with Warwick in a bid to restore Henry VI to the throne of England. I bring to mind when Edward and I had to escape to Burgundy, where our sister Margaret, our dear sister now Duchess of Burgundy, with her husband Charles the Bold, gave us shelter and protection. George had married Warwick's elder daughter Isabel, I know that Anne was absolutely distraught to think that Edward had shunned her father, after all he had done for him. And she thought that she would never see me again now. I must admit that I also felt the same and wondered if our paths would ever cross again. It was like the wheel of fortune had turned completely round. My father and brother had been killed and now the love of my life, my beautiful childhood sweetheart Anne Neville seemed to be lost to me forever.

With Charles and Margaret's help we managed to raise a small force and to return to England and try take back what we had lost. Never will I forget Barnet, It was Easter Sunday, day of all days, this had to be the worst possible day to fight a battle on. I was just eighteen years old, Edward had given me command of the vanguard, this was my first major battle. Although I had fought before in minor engagements mostly in Wales, this was very different, I knew that we would be up against some of the best trained and disciplined men in England, not to mention people like Warwick himself. Edward had trusted me like no one else and I had to make myself worthy of his trust.

I had prayed to God to restore the throne to its rightful place as the House of York.

A huge thick belt of fog hung over the battlefield, it came to meet my men like a thick blanket enveloping them as we moved forward. And then the engagement, it seemed like we had just hit the wall of hell itself: the thrusts, the clamour of steel on steel, the cries of men all around, the smell of blood and death. We were floundering in the darkness and the fog and at times it was nigh on in possible to make out friend from foe. To my left and just behind me, my squire went down was instantly killed, almost immediately I was cut in the leg, but managed to retain my balance and cut down the assailant. The fog closed in on us and for a moment we could see nothing. I called out to my men, "For the King and for York, to me men to me." I was losing blood I could feel the sticky goo running down my leg, I felt light headed. This was not the time to weaken, not now. I could just make out a rise in the ground and panting called again to my men. "For England and St. George!"

We made the rise and now we could see above the fog belt. We could see Barnet, the town, the buildings. Warwick's men were relentless, but we held our ground amidst hail after hail of arrow storms and little by little won the day. At the end of it, I heard that Richard Neville Earl Warwick had been killed in battle. This was a sad day indeed for me, although I was grateful to Almighty God for his great mercy on a Yorkist victory. I had hoped that maybe Warwick "The Kingmaker" would be spared. He was my mentor and father figure for many years and he was a gallant knight. He was also Anne's farther, may he rest in the arms of our Lord Jesus Christ Amen.

In the chapel I suddenly heard a noise which brought me back from my thoughts and prayers. I turned around to see Anne standing behind me. I had not noticed her, or heard her come in, up to this point. How long she had been there I cannot say. She put her arms around me and knelt down to where I was and took my face into her hands.

"My Lord, My Dickon, you are much troubled; tell me. You have been here now for much of the night, what is it Richard?" She saw that my eyes were wet and kissed them.

"I cannot, my love, it is well now you are here."

We knelt there together, just hugging one another. Anne seemed to understand my very thoughts.

"My Lord, you are so very cold, come, I hear the maids, we must bathe and dress it is time that we broke our fast."

It was during these times that I preferred to be away from London and court, up to my beloved northern counties, where I could be my own self and not have to get involved with politics. Home to Middleham, where Anne and I could come home to see our family once again, little Ned, Kathryn and John. And, as always, the very warm welcome of the people of Yorkshire, who I did miss when we had to go to London. Edward had made me Commander of the North and so a great amount of my time was spent keeping the borders safe from Scottish invasion and fighting to take back towns like Berwick on Tweed.

Chapter Two
Bestwood Park Nottingham
April 1484

Anne and I are out hunting in Bestwood (Beskwood) Park, Francis was to come along with us, but, at the last moment, some unforeseen local business came up that needed urgent attention. Francis had volunteered to stay behind and help deal with it. In fact I think that Anne and Francis had concocted the whole thing, so that we could be together and out of the castle for a while. We have a very small party with us and are staying at Bestwood lodge, which Anne always likes to stray in. She says it is far more welcoming than the castle, although we both enjoy being at the castle, but most times we do not have so much time to ourselves as we would like. Anne is cantering out in front of me, she has chosen to ride her favourite Palfrey, which has an amazing turn of speed and can stop on a coin if need be. Anne just loves to hunt; she always has been a natural rider, even as a child in Middleham. I guess the dales are an excellent place to learn about hunting and riding and she was invariably one of the front riders, much to the countess's disapproval. She often scolded Anne for being not lady like; a well-bred lady should always let the gentlemen in the hunt take the lead, she would say. But she took little heed. I was riding one of the coursers borrowed from the lodge, as my old favourite White Surrey had thrown a shoe and in any case properly was not totally suited to close hunting here in Bestwood, as he was a destrier, far more used to open battlefields. The weather was good, even though it was still early in the year; it really was so beautiful out there in the woods. The hunt master had spotted something out to our left, we gave chase; Anne had to turn her palfrey quite sharply and I held my breath as she cut in front of us. But she was on to it, a huge boar, a fine specimen of an animal. I shouted to her to rein back and let it have its head, but Anne was having none of it. Just a little way up ahead the vegetation closed in on both sides and I could see where the beast was making for, there was barely enough room to ride a horse through, so, to my horror, Anne jumped down from her steed, spear in hand and started to make her way through the dense vegetation. "No, Anne! No!" I hailed, as we too dismounted and ran to scramble after her. There was a noise, which I knew only too well, comes when a boar is cornered and has nowhere to go. It will stand and fight often to the death and sometimes that of its assailant.

"Anne! No! For God's sake back off."

The huge hog shifted its eyes for just a second as I approached and grabbed her and managed to pull her back and to one side, leaving enough room for the boar to make an escape through the undergrowth. As it sped past us, it tore into the hunt master hurtling him to the ground and gashing his side with one of his enormous tusks.

"My sweet love, are you hurt?"

I could see that Anne was in a state of some shock and had gone a deathly shade of pale by this time. The rest of the party had now caught with up with us, "See to the hunt master." I shouted, as I settled Anne down on the stump of an old oak tree.

"I am not hurt bad, my liege," came back the reply from the hunt master. "See to the Lady Anne."

I called for some wine to settle her and we sat for some time there.

"I am so sorry, Dickon, I was so taken up with chasing the beast that I gave little thought to the consequences."

"My love, it matters not, I give thanks that all are well and we live to hunt another day."

Francis joined us for dinner at Bestwood lodge and as we ate, Anne was retelling Francis her tale of the huge boar on the hunt, which I have to say at this point had become very much larger. Tomorrow we return to the castle to welcome both John and Kathryn to stay with us. After the meal and tables are cleared, we sit by the welcoming fire in the great hall and with flagons of some very good wine. Francis brings up the subject of Kathryn's future.

"There is talk of a betrothal to William Herbert, Earl of Huntingdon. She is a beautiful young lady with a keen interest in lots of subjects, Dickon, and would make a prize for any suitor."

"Kate is still yet young and just turned fourteen, I would have her with us a while longer," I say. "And Herbert can wait until she is ready."

Anne was staring into the fire and I guessed what she was thinking. "Is it Ned my love?"

"Aye it is, Richard, I was just thinking how nice it will be to see him once again, to hear all he has to say about his lessons. But also about how well he is keeping. Oh Richard, can we make our way to Middleham for just a short while, I long to see him and hold him again?"

"Yes, my love, I also, but we have to finish our progress, then, God be willing, we will make our way as planned to Middleham, I promise you this."

The next morning sees us on our way back to Nottingham Castle, it seems more bustling and busy than ever. John has already arrived and has settled himself in after his journey from Middleham Castle. Immediately Anne runs and greats him, "Dear John, how are you?" John makes an elegant bow to her and kisses her hand.

"Oh, John, I forget that you are growing up now." She makes a curtsey back to him.

"Thank you, my mother Lady Anne, I am very well and all the more so for seeing you."

"Richard, I do believe your son is trying to flirt with me."

"And why not indeed, is not my Queen the most beautiful lady in all the realm? What say you, Johnny? You have been away too long and we have missed your company, you are most welcome."

John bows to me, "My King and liege lord, my father,

I have missed you all so much."

"Enough of this, Johnny, come here and give your father a hug."

I realise as we hug one another how much I do miss my family these days and just how much they do mean to me. I order wine to be brought and can see that Anne is just wanting to ask about young Ned. "Well, Anne, ask John what you have been wanting to ask since he came in the room."

"Thank you, Richard, I guess you must know what I would ask you John, and that is, how is our young Edward Prince of Wales?"

John looked at Anne and then at Richard, wondering what to say and how to begin. "My good mother Lady Anne, Ned is very much the same as he has been now for some time, that is to say, he seems not to be any the worst for his ills and Anne Idley watches over him like a shepherd watches over his flock. As I was preparing to leave for Nottingham, he gave me this note for you both, on which he has written and also included some illuminations, which he hopes you might enjoy. The good doctor says to tell you that he continues to look after him and with the Lord's help he may recover to full health again. I know that Ned longs for the day when you will make your way back to Middleham again."

Richard takes the letter and breaks the seal. Anne hovers at his side, together they read.

'My Lady Mother and Lord Father, I miss you both so very much, as of late I have not been able to go outside of the castle here, because Anne Idley and the doctor say that the weather is yet too damp for me to venture far. But when it picks up they may let me go outside, I just cannot wait to ride my pony again, I did go down to the stables to see him the just the other day.

'He looks in fine condition, John and I have been spending a lot of time together, although he has other duties, he comes to me each day and we talk or play chess. My studies go well, I can hold a conversation now in French, but I still struggle with my Latin. My tutor says that it will come given time. I hope that you both like my illuminations. God bless you, Mother and Father, and please hurry home to Middleham and to me as soon as you can do. Your loving and obedient Edward.'

"Richard my lord, do you think that we may be able to travel to Middleham quite soon?"

"Yes, my love, I have yet to finish some matters here, which should take no more than a few days. Then we will make haste up to Middleham."

The next day Kathryn arrives to join them from London. Anne receives her in her solar. "My lady Kathryn, you are most welcome, how well you do look."

Kathryn curtseys low and takes Anne's outstretched hands. "My Lady mother, it is so good to see you again, you also are looking well, my Queen."

Anne dismisses her ladies, and orders some wine.

"Come, Kathryn, we have much to talk about." She offers Kathryn a seat by the fire. "Your Father and Francis have gone into the town to meet with the Lord Mayor. Knowing Francis, he will no doubt persuade your Father that they are in need of some refreshments in 'Ye Olde Trip to Jerusalem' if I am not mistaken. So it may be a while before they return. Now, Kathryn, how are you really, are you happy at court in London and do they treat you well?"

"Yes, Mother, on the whole, I think that I am respected well enough. Although it may be because of my father's influence as King more than anything that I say or do. Lady Anne my mother, may I ask a question of you?"

"Of course you may Kathryn, do not be afraid to ask me anything, is there something that troubles you my dear?"

"The question does not trouble me so much, as to make me wonder if it be true. There is talk around court that my father is looking for a suitor for me and he is looking at Sir William Herbert Earl of Huntington. Is it true, my mother, and is he a good man, for I do not know him?"

"Be at ease, Kathryn, Richard would never make a decision about such an important issue as to your marriage without first talking to you. He may be King, but he is your father and loves you very much, as I do. You are the daughter that I never had and would always do my best for you.

"I know that Richard believes that you are not yet old enough for marriage and that he would like to keep you with us for some time yet. Having said that, William Herbert may indeed be a good match for you, Kathryn, but one that has not yet arisen. So put your mind at rest, if and when the situation does arise you will be the first to know, that I promise you. Does that answer your question my dear?" Kathryn gets up and puts her arms around Anne.

"Thank you, my mother, I love you."

Chapter Three
Nottingham Castle
April 1484

Dark Days

Richard had sent to London for Elizabeth to come and join us at Nottingham, Bess as he liked to call her. Bess was his favourite niece and she was also one of my most attentive ladies at court. A very well liked young lady and a very beautiful one, a quality which she almost certainly inherited from her mother. But, unlike her mother, Bess was a very amenable and pleasant young lady and in this respect did not take after the Woodvilles at all. She was never happier than when she was helping to make our life easier, in whatever way she could. And would ask nothing in return.

Often were the times when Richard was away with his duties that she would come and sit with me, after my ladies had retired for the night. We would talk, play cards, or chess, even read together. When we were home in Middleham there was often a real family gathering. With John, Kathryn, Edward, Elizabeth and of course, Francis Lovell, William Catesby and Richard Ratcliffe. And very often many more. These were very happy times when we could all just relax without the normal court pressures in London. So we are here in Nottingham Castle at the moment, with our children and friends around us. The one person missing, of course, is Edward and we worry continually about him, we all miss him a great deal. Although I loved and cared a great deal about Richard's other two children John and Kathryn, which he had fathered before our marriage. Edward of course was my only child with Richard and because of that was very special to me and I know to Richard also.

Richard and the court had gone into town, at the Mayor's invitation for a special civic celebration to be held in the guildhall. I was not feeling too good on this day and at the last minute asked if I could be excused from attending. Richard was immediately concerned about me, but after reassuring him that I would be fine and maybe it would be beneficial to have some peace and quiet for a while he had said that I should rest. After all it had been quite a busy last few days for us. Kate wanted to stay with me and see to my needs, but I sent her and my ladies off with the rest of the party.

After they had gone, I went for a walk around the castle battlements, which I hoped may clear my head a little. The views from up here I had always admired, the sky seemed to go on forever, the countryside and the huge forests of Sherwood, the bustling town of Nottingham just below. It was one of those clear still days that you sometimes get at this time of the year. The castle was indeed quiet, except up there for the occasional guards who seemed surprised to see me and bowed as I passed by.

But still I could not settle, as now sitting at my embroidery I cannot explain it, but just feel very uneasy. In the end I put a side my work and wander down to where I can hear voices coming from the huge castle kitchens.

The cooks and kitchen maids are hard at work preparing dinner for this evening, they are as astonished to see me as the guards had been and immediately stop work and curtsey.

"Please do not stop work I have not come to intrude on you."

One of the cooks comes forward and asks, "Are you well, my lady, please sit down here." She sends one of the maids to fetch a small ale for me.

"Do I indeed look Ill?" I ask, knowing not quite what to say.

She answers, "Perhaps a little pale, my lady."

After a while I take my leave and thank them for their kindness.

I wander out into the gardens which are now becoming beautiful again after the long winter. The gardeners are busy planting out flowers that will bloom later on and are also at work in the herb garden taking out plants that have been lost due to the hard frosts this winter. It is pleasant here in the spring sunshine and I find a seat in a secluded spot where the birds are singing. Soon my mind starts to fill with memories from the past, being in the French court of Queen Margaret of Anjou that Angevin women when we had to beg from King Louis, exile with our family and George Duke of Clarence. Of how Margaret despised and treated us and insulted us at every opportunity. How eventfully Louis came up with the idea of an alliance with Margaret to beat the Yorkist cause; to take back England and reinstall King Henry VI back on the throne once more. As much as my father the Earl detested the idea of having to form an alliance with that woman, as he called her, Louis would have it no other way. And for Warwick to get back to England with an army and money it was the only way. I have never seen my father brought so low as he was then, Warwick the mighty Kingmaker, second at one time only to the King himself, to have to come to this.

Margaret was furious and would not accept the terms that Louis offered her, even though it meant that if Warwick was successful, Edward, her beloved son, Edward Lancaster and Westminster, Prince of Wales, would be elevated to inherit the throne on the death of his father Henry VI, as Louis put it to her. In the end King Louis gave Margaret no alternative but to accept the terms of an alliance with Warwick, and very begrudgingly by both sides the deal was done. However, unbeknownst to me, part of this deal by Louis and my father was that I should be betrothed to Edward Lancaster Queen Margaret's son and Prince of Wales. I was heartbroken, I had only spoken to him twice since we had been in France; he was a self-seeking, conceited upstart, full of his own importance. And besides this I did not love or care for him, my love was for my Dickon, wherever he may be now God only may know. I did want to become his "Lady Anne, Princess of Wales" thank you very much. My mother The Countess, spoke to me in no uncertain terms, although kindly, "You are a Neville and will behave as such, your father has tried to do the very best he can for you, do not let him down. One day, God be the willing, you may become Queen of England."

So, on Tuesday 13th December 1470, in Angers Cathedral with just twelve days to go before Christmas, we were married, the Prince in the finest cloth of gold, the black and red of his heraldic ostrich feather on his tunic. The rich ermine of my cloak I cared nothing for at all and would have exchanged it in a moment to be with Richard.

But the worst humiliation was yet to come, on that wedding day, when we had been married before God, Queen Margaret refused to let her son consummate the marriage.

Saying that she had kept her part of the bargain and looked for better things for her son, she kept me in her court as Princess of Wales, but I was never allowed to be alone with the Prince for one moment.

Later on when we heard that my father the Earl was killed on that Easter Day at the Battle of Barnet, I was distraught to think that so mighty a warrior could be cut down; it was unthinkable to me. The Kingmaker was no more.

Afterwards, when we sailed to England with the rest of our army and met with the Yorkist army at Tewksbury, I just had the worst feeling about it. Although my husband seemed full of confidence, news came to us later on in the day that it had gone badly for us and it was a complete Yorkist victory. My husband, Edward Lancaster Prince of Wales, was dead. I did feel sorrow for him, after all he was my husband. But somehow a sense of relieve also. After this, Margaret had no further interest or use for me; I was as nothing to her.

Still sitting on the seat in the garden in Nottingham Castle, I had not realised how long I had been there, wrapped up in my thoughts and memories as I had been.

Strangely now I did feel much better and was ready to face my dear Dickon and the rest of the court on their return to the castle. At dinner everyone seemed to be in good spirits and afterwards when all had dined. Richard lead me in a progress dance followed by all the others. When we came close, he whispered in my ear so as not to attract attention, "I love you, my sweetheart, how lucky I am to have a lady that is beautiful and caring. And how lucky is England to have a Queen that is so dedicated to her King and country as you as are, my lady, God bless you." And with that he takes me in his arms and kisses me on the lips, with his warm passion. I can feel the blood stir within me and feel my face burn with the heat.

All I can manage in return of his complements is to say that, "I love you, Richard my King, and my husband."

What I do not say, perhaps because Francis has intervened and whisked me off in the progress with a sly grin on his face, is that I am the most lucky person in all of England. To have someone like Richard and how lucky is England to have a King like Richard.

Richard and Francis are hearing petitions in the Great Hall with a good number of people being present on this day. All at once the great doors swing open and in come riders looking as if they have just ridden for their lives, covered in mud and dust. Preceded by a messenger, equally dirty and muddy, and King Richard's steward.

They drop to their knees in front of Richard; his steward stands and asks the messenger to come forward.

"My lord these men have ridden for many hours and bring you some very bad news indeed," the messenger looks from the steward to Richard and Francis and back to the steward, not knowing just how to impart what he has to say.

"Well man speak up, I would hear your message."

"My lord, I can say this no other way. The Prince of Wales is dead; your son is dead. He died yesterday and we have ridden all through the night to let you know."

The steward handed Richard a velum scroll tied in great haste, not even sealed. "This is from Doctor Hobbys my lord."

Richard collapsed into his chair and handed the scroll to Francis. "Read it Francis, for God's sake please read it." His mind was swimming, this was a mistake, it had to be a mistake, dear Lord Jesus, not Edward, please not Edward. The Hall had gone quiet and still as a mouse being chased by a cat just before it pounces. Francis opened the scroll with shaking hands and read the contents.

"Francis read me what it says."

"My King and liege Lord, it is with the up most regret that I have to inform you that The Prince of Wales died this very night, Isabel Burgh sent to fetch me as his breathing was getting laboured. I tried every way to increase his level of breathing, but in the end to no avail. He died peacefully in the arms of Anne Idley and Isabel Burgh. The priest gave him his last rights just before he passed. Mass is being said for him as I write this. May The Good Lord Jesus Christ give him rest and Peace. Your servant, William Hobby's."

"How do I tell Anne and the children, Francis?" Richard asked after some time had passed and the court had been dismissed.

Now the castle took on an eerie silence, as if everyone had suddenly disappeared. "Dickon, the only way to tell it, is as it is. You cannot hold it from them, they will now know very quickly, from other sources. Better it comes from you."

Chapter Four
Middleham Castle
1484

My poor Ned, he has been buried just a few weeks now. We made our way as quickly as we could, from Nottingham up to Middleham. Although Anne was in no condition to make the journey at all. She was thin and pale, would not eat of much and slept little if at all. But she insisted on coming. I had arranged for her to travel in a litter, but she refused, saying that it would slow us up and wanted to make great haste to be with Edward before the funeral ceremony took place. I looked at her often as we travelled; her eyes seemed to be fixed straight in front of her, looking neither to left or right. Many were the times that I just wanted to stop and scoop her up in my arms, but she seemed to ignore everything, other than the will to keep on going as fast as possible. And many were the times that I had to force her to stop and rest the horses; she would just have kept going, perfectly obvious to everything else.

I had considered for Ned to be buried, firstly at St. Mary and Alkelda Middleham, where I had set up a collegiate church and installed a dean. And secondly, maybe, York Minster, as was befitting a Prince of the realm. But Anne would have none of it; she implored me to let him be buried in St. Helen and The Holy Cross Sheriff Hutton. In the Neville chapel, wherein Anne put it, he would be near to his Neville family. And near enough to Sheriff Hutton Castle and to Middleham, the area he loved in his lifetime on this earth. I just had not the heart to refuse Anne, after all she had been through and it did make a lot of sense. So it was arranged that when we were getting near, that the cortège would come out from Middleham to meet us at Sheriff Hutton. And then we would form up and make our way to the church in procession, to do great honour to our dear son Ned,

Edward of Middleham. Prince of Wales. Duke of Cornwall. Earl of Salisbury. Earl of Chester.

Dear Lord Jesus keep him in your tender loving care, he was a brave and obedient Prince, who never harmed anyone. Amen.

Returning to Middleham late one evening, I saw that there was a light in Edward's tower. My first thought was that it may be Anne, although she had not yet brought herself to venture there since Ned's death, as this had been his quarters. Master Hampton our old and faithful steward, was waiting for me.

"Welcome, my Lord, I have a message from the Queen, to say that she has retired to bed and had arranged for food to be left for me in the great hall."

As I walked inside I remembered the light in the tower and questioned Master Hampton about it.

"Sorry, my Lord, but I had not noticed anyone up there, I will send for it to be checked out immediately."

"No, please do not concern yourself, Master Hampton, I will see to it myself, I would stretch my legs after being long in the saddle this day."

"Is there anything else I can do for you, my Lord?"

"No thank you, you may dismiss everyone now, I will serve myself."

"As you wish, my Lord."

Richard made his way to the tower, with a number of thoughts running through his head, it had been a long and tiring day. But how he did love coming home to his castle in Middleham and to his beloved Anne. He loved her as he had never loved another living soul, save that of his children, of whom dear Ned now lay buried in Sheriff Hutton. The grief that we both felt was like a torment beyond endurance at times. And as he approached the battlements which ran across towards Edward's tower, and marvelled at the bright starry sky, Richard remembered once again coming to this castle as a nine year old, to be mentored by Warwick the Kingmaker who had been his cousin. Such a lot had happened since then, the happiest years of his life had been spent within these walls. This had been his home for the past eleven years, this where he had first brought his beautiful wife Anne after having been married for just over a week, and also now where his dear son Edward had died, with neither he nor Anne being able to be at his bedside at his end. The light shone brightly from the tower. Now just a little way ahead.

Richard could now hear voices as he approached with some trepidation as to the meaning of this, especially at this hour. He opened the door to find both John and Kathryn on their knees beside Edward's bed, both of them in tears and Kathryn holding John to try and comfort him. At the sight of Richard, they just ran into his arms, forgetting all protocol and he hugged them close for what seemed like an age, until their sobbing ceased. "Forgive us, my father my Lord, we meant no harm, we just felt that we needed to be where Edward had spent the last hours of his short life on earth. And say a prayer for him here."

At this, Richard could no longer hold back his tears and the three of them fell to their knees, hands held, while they prayed as they never prayed before, for the blessed soul of little Ned, Prince of Wales.

Chapter Five
Scarborough Castle
July 1484

We have made a detour on our road north to York, to come and spend a few days at one of Anne and Ned's favourite Castles on the east coast of Yorkshire, Scarborough.

I just thought that it might pick Anne up a little, with some good sea air and wonderful views. Anne is concerning me of late, it is now some eleven weeks since little Ned passed away, and she is still not eating or sleeping well, she is grieving badly, as we all are. But my love just will not let it go, she blames herself for not being there for him and although the good doctor Hobbys tells her that it would not have made any difference in the end, she will not accept it.

I see her growing thinner by the day and have all sorts of food prepared to try and tempt her, but she just picks at it. Bess has taken on the role of nurse to Anne, as they do get on well together and sees to her every need. Anne will no longer share my bed, as she does not want to disturb me, as she tends only to sleep for small amounts of time and spends hours on her knees in the chapel. This is tearing me apart, I do not know what to do, what can I do?

Every evening I go to her bedchamber, and we talk or play chess, sometimes I read to her, but she tires quickly and when Bess has put her to bed and seen to her needs, I just sit and stroke her head as she drifts into an unsteady sort of sleep, then kiss her on her forehead. It is breaking my heart to see her like this. My love, my beautiful wife, I have to leave as tears start to form in my eyes. Dear Lord Jesus what can I do for her?

With Bess's help and with the good air, Anne does seem to be a little better, and is even eating small amounts of food, but she is still very melancholy most of the time. We stand looking out over the beautiful bay, I hold her around her now slender waist, I pull her lips to mine and we kiss as we have not done for some time.

"Anne I have only ever loved you, for as far as I can ever remember, my love, and would lay down my life for you if needs be."

"I know, my dearest, my sweet Dickon, I know. You will never ever know just how much you mean to me, you are my life. Without you there is now nothing for me and I love you dearly. But sometimes I think that you may be better off without me, as I am such a drain on you."

"Do not ever say that, Anne, I could not go on without you."

And with that I just scoop her up and we go indoors and up to her bedchamber.

Chapter Six
The North
July 1484

We spend the summer mainly in the north, going to the council of the north at Sandal Castle, which is now always a reminder to me of what happened there with that vile witch, Margaret of Anjou, and the butchery of my father and brother.

And then on to York, ah York, it is always such a welcome pleasure to be back in York. But again it does now hurt Anne and myself to think that just a short while ago, we were celebrating here with Edward at his investiture as Prince of Wales.

Anne seems to be somewhat better in health nowadays, but when I look at her, I see that she is not quite the Neville I used to know. And I still need to encourage her to eat properly. The new repairs have been commissioned at the castle and work has begun on the Minster College, so at last I can see some progress taking place,

We do the rounds of our properties here and go from castle to castle, then back home to Middleham. The monument to Edward, has been erected in Sheriff Hutton church, it is so like him and Anne just completely broke down. I must confess that I really fought to hold back the tears, but knew that if I let go it would make it even worse for Anne.

After a few days I needed to return to Westminster, so I took John with me and left Francis Lovell and Rob Percy to see to things here, along with Bess and Anne's Ladies to keep her company. Anne came down to the stables to see us off, I could tell she had been crying.

"Please Richard, must you really go now?"

"Yes, my love, it is important that I go, but I will be back just as soon as I can, take care of yourself for me." As I mounted White Surrey Anne held my free hand, as if she would never let go.

I bent down and kissed her full on the mouth, not caring what my squires and escort would think. As we rode out over the drawbridge, I looked back and could see her standing on the entrance steps, waving her white kerchief. She looked so lonely standing there, it just tore at my heart. I looked at John and saw that he felt it, too. "Let's away, my son, the sooner we are there, the sooner back, what say you?"

"Aye, Father." And with that we dug in our heels and headed south and for London.

When we returned to Middleham some days later, the household turned out to welcome us back. The business in London had been concluded much sooner than expected, no doubt spurred on by the urge to get back to Anne and home.

Anne stood on the steps to the entrance more or less as I had left her and it made me wonder if she had actually moved in all the time we had been away. As the days passed we settled in to a routine of life which was very pleasing. Hunting was always the thing that I enjoyed being part of, but these days Anne did not accompany us, which I did miss an awful lot. Instead she would walk in the gardens with her ladies and they would sit and read on fine days, or if not she would be found in her solar embroidering perhaps a new altar piece for the churches in Middleham or Sheriff Hutton. Time went by so quickly, whenever we would ride out, with the boar displayed on the livery of my men and on our banners, local people would stop and cheer us. Anne would say,

"The people do love you so, Dickon."

Chapter Seven
Westminster London
Christmas 1484

It is a few days before Christmas and we have come to Westminster to prepare for the celebrations. Although I have to say that celebrating is the last thing on my mind at the moment, Anne is now most clearly very ill. It pains me to see her so, she is trying so very hard to put a brave face on things and will not give in. But she fools no one, especially me, she coughs a great deal and spits into a kerchief, which she carries with her. She turns away from me so that I may not see what is in the kerchief, but I know, I have seen this before, it is blood, not bright red, but dark in colour. Anne has asked doctor Hobbys not to tell me, but I cornered him coming out from the Queens rooms and demanded he tell me as much as he knows. He was strained, but told me that in his opinion the Queen has consumption and that from now on I am not to sleep or to make any physical contact with her, for my own protection.

"Great God, Hobbys, you do not know what you ask of me?"

"My Lord, I cannot stress this enough, because you could become ill too."

"Hobbys, what is to be done?"

"Sire, I have ordered an elixir which should help and also sleeping drafts to help the Queen sleep at nights, she should get as much fresh air as possible, which may be difficult here in London. And I know that the Queen would never consent to leaving you here, my Lord. Truth be known, sire, she does know now that she is very ill, without me saying anything and may not pull through."

"My precious Jesus, Hobbys, how long, man, how long?"

"Sire, that is the most difficult question to answer, but under present circumstances, if you would press me to answer, I may say a matter of just a few months at most."

I sink to my chair, unable to comprehend fully what the doctor has said. "Hobbys does the Queen know?"

"Yes, my Lord, she knows, not that I have said it, but she knows well enough and just wants to spend her last days on this earth with you, sire. She is a most remarkable Lady."

"Thank you, Doctor Hobbys, do what you can for her to make her comfortable, please."

"Of course, my Lord, I will do everything in my power to make sure she is well looked after."

After the good doctor leaves I write straight away to ask Elizabeth Woodville if she will once again send Bess to care for Anne and pass on what the doctor has said.

Then I go to the chapel to pray, "Lord Jesus Christ, how can this be, what have I done that is so wrong to justify your wrath, on me? My father and brother killed at Wakefield, My brother the King, cut off in his prime, my dear little Ned dead and now Anne is fatally ill. Lord, must it be this way? What can I do to make amends?" After a while I hear the Priest come in, I must have been here for quite some time, as it was daylight when I entered and now it is dark.

"My Lord, are you well? The Queen is asking for you."

So I go to Anne in her bedchamber, not knowing what I will say to her or how to face her. She is lying propped up in bed, she looks so thin and small in this huge bed. I kneel by her and kiss her forehead.

"My Lord, you should not be on your knees to me, but I to you. You know, Dickon, how do know, was it Hobbys, I told him to say nothing of it to you?"

"My dearest sweetest love, I had to know for sure, do not blame Hobbys, I did but force him to tell me in all truth. But you will return to full health again, I swear it."

"No Richard, No my dear, Dickon, it cannot be so, you must be strong now for both of us and help me to overcome my fears. Oh, Richard my love I am so much afraid, please help me."

I take her in my arms and tears from my face run down on to her nightclothes. "Please my love, you must not hold me, has not the doctor told you so?"

"Yes he has told me in no uncertain terms, I just do not care, Anne my love, I will hold you and be near to you and if the good Lord deigns it so that I am become ill, then so be it."

"Thank you, Richard, for I am so very blessed in having such wonderful caring husband."

We talked together holding one another for a very long time. Of the many things that Anne said, one was that we would keep the Christmas festivities and celebrations and make them really special this time. Eventually she slept in my arms and I lay down beside her and watched her sleeping, until I also fell asleep. The twelve-night feast and masque was to be a huge celebration, but I was concerned for Anne that she may not be up to it. She did want it to go ahead as planned, I have to marvel now at where she did manage to get her strength from and at times she would whisper to me, "Richard, take my hand my love." And in the end I doubt if many people did notice that there was anything wrong at all.

Early in the New Year Bess came to us and fussed about Anne, making sure that whenever I could not be with her or was away, that she was in her company.

Doctor Hobbys made frequent visits to check on Anne and reported little change in her condition, except to say that she did mostly seem in better spirits.

Whenever we could, we walk in the gardens at Westminster, which Anne loved and were a delight at this time of the year. Many of the spring plants were beginning to show themselves. Sometimes we had the company of Kate and John on these walks, we would stroll and talk, but always Anne would take my hand and lean on me, so as to not make it obvious that she was finding it difficult to walk unaided.

More and more often now she would have bouts of coughing followed by turning away and spewing into her kerchief. And was having to spend long periods resting, just to try and regain her strength.

Chapter Eight
Windsor Castle
January/February 1485

Mid-January, Richard moved his court from Westminster to Windsor, in the hope that maybe the air and surroundings would benefit Anne. She had always preferred Windsor to Westminster. But it became apparent as the month wore on that she was slowly getting worse and that her strength was weakening.

Shortly before Candlemas, Doctor Hobbys ordered her to bed and Richard realised then that he could no longer hold back the truth which he had known from the beginning of Anne's illness. She would never see another spring on this earth with him.

Richard now reserved the evenings for Anne, he would go to her bedchamber and they would play chess or Richard would read to her, she had always enjoyed him reading to her, but as the days passed by he found that she seemed not to be able to concentrate for any length of time. So he would just hold her and stroke her head until she fell asleep.

February came in with biting cold winds and snow, one evening after leaving Anne, I made my way to St. George's Chapel and was reminded that it needed finishing. Brother Edward had started it almost ten years earlier, it was a magnificent building. He walked up to where Edward had been placed in his tomb and stood before it, then, as he approached the altar, fell to his knees. "In Nomine Patris et Filii Spiritus Sancti," he prayed for Anne, and for his dear brother Edward, for Ned and for his Children, prayed that they would never have to face the things he had to face.

And at last he came away.

Chapter Nine
Westminster
March 1485

The Sky Darkens

The court has moved back now to Westminster, I had wanted to leave Anne undisturbed in Windsor, but she had wanted to be near to me and so I had her transported back in a litter slowly to her quarters here. Bess has been a real comfort to Anne, spending long hours with her. On one of my evening visits Bess was with her and she had been crying, but on my entrance she curtseyed and made to go.

"Do not leave Bess."

"Nay, I must, my Lord," she said and almost ran out of the Queen's chamber.

"My sweetheart, how are you this evening?"

"Richard, I am not for long now."

Richard took her hand, "My dearest love, you must not say that please, do not say that."

"My Dickon, dearest love, I have to tell you."

"No, Anne, you will get better yet. I will take care of you."

"Hush, my love, all my happiness that I have ever known has come from you, I have loved you from when we were young and you have made me your Queen and given me of our son Edward, whom I shall be with very soon now. We will look down on you and bless you and keep you safe."

Richard could not hold back his tears any longer, he just fell into her arms.

"Richard, please, I have made my peace with The Lord Jesus Christ and asked him to watch over you and guide you in everything you do. Please pray for me, my darling, I shall wait for you and one day we will be together again, all three of us."

Just before daybreak on Wednesday 16th March 1485 Anne Neville Queen of England received the last rites of the Roman Catholic Church. At midday she passed peacefully away with her beloved Richard by her bedside holding her hand to the last. All at once a great darkness swept over the land as if to mark her passing.

Chapter Ten
Nottingham Castle
Richard's Castle of Care

June 1485

I have just received a sealed letter from my dear sister
Margaret in Burgundy; she has reliable information that
the Tudor is gathering his forces together in Harfleur.

'Richard, Greetings, you would want to know if you
do not already, that the Tudor is preparing to sail and is
gathering his forces in Harfleur. We estimate that he
may have between two to three thousand men, mostly
French mercenaries, not including Lancastrians that
have been here with him in exile of course, such as
Oxford and Jasper Tudor. He has been given cannon and
gold also, so he may be able to recruit when he lands. I
hope that this information helps you, my dear brother,
to deal with this welsh upstart. Signed: Margaret
Duchess of Burgundy.'

I show the letter to John Kendall my chief Secretary.
"Does this tie in with what we already know of the
Tudor John?"
"Yes, my Lord, our scouts are saying just that."
"Very well then, John, call a full meeting of the
council for the morrow."

"Yes, my Lord."

As Richard sits in the council meeting, he looks around the chamber and is heartened to see most of his friends have made it. Men like Francis Lovell, John Howard, William Catesby, John de la pole, Richard Ratcliffe, and John Scrope.

"Gentlemen, I bid you all a good day, as you know we have for some time now been receiving reports of the Tudor's activities abroad, it seems that these may now be coming to a head. It is understood that his rag tag army is gathering in Harfleur. Gentlemen, I propose that we move to Nottingham and await development there, it should be much easier to strike out from there to wherever he decides to make for, and therefore we may be able to stop him in his tracks. What think you, Gentlemen?"

Francis is one of the first to reply. "My Lord, have we any information at all as to where he might make for?"

John Howard cuts in, "He will not try to land in the north, he has no friends there and would have a rough time of it."

"My Lord, says Richard Ratcliff, he may try his luck in Wales, claiming his Welsh ancestry and he would maybe as like pick up large numbers of support on the way."

"You may be right, Ratcliffe, however my hope in Wales is that William Herbert or Rhys ap Thomas will stop him and if not then he must make for Shrewsbury where he will not pass and we can move to crush him.

"So then, Gentlemen, do we move to Nottingham?"

"Aye, my Lord, we do."

"Nottingham Castle always feels welcoming and friendly to me and I am most happy to be here. Although it also holds some very sad memories, it was here that we received the news of dear Ned's passing and I see Anne in every part of this place. But I know that by being here, we are best placed to strike out at Tudor wherever he may land.

"Thomas Stanley has been summoned to meet us here, he is my one big concern in these plans to finally put the Tudor down. The Stanleys were ever slippery eels and God knows at this time I do need them. But Stanley will be weighing up all his options, especially with Margaret Beaufort as his wife, will he then through in his lot and back Tudor hoping for greater rewards than I can give him, I know not at this point. The Beauforts have been ever a thorn in the house of York, some say that I should have, and still should, execute Margaret for her treachery and I know that she has been communicating and trying to raise both money and support for the Tudor, even after the first failed invasion by him. I did think that Thomas Stanley would hold her in check. I now know that not to be true,

"However, I will not make war on women and to an extent I can have some sympathy for Margaret, in that she has had a very difficult life. Having the Tudor when she was just thirteen and I have even heard it said, maybe twelve years old.

"After losing three husbands, she has had to fight to do what most mothers would do, keep herself and her son safe over many years. We must try and get the Stanleys to commit for us.

"My other big concern is, of course, Northumberland, Henry Percy. I have also summoned him; he seems so aloof nowadays, maybe he still broods about the death of his father at Towton. He is always very hard to read and I must admit I cannot work out what he wants, but hopefully he will be with us."

During a quiet time one day in my rooms, I talk to John de la Pole, Earl of Lincoln. "Jack, I need to talk to you alone."

"What is it, my Lord Uncle?"

"Jack, if and when this Tudor invasion takes place I want you as far away from the action as possible, do you understand me?"

"No, my Lord, I do not understand your meaning, I am your loyal nephew and I would fight at your side."

"I know that you are loyal, Jack, but I am not asking. Think about it, Jack, you are so much more than the Earl of Lincoln and my nephew. I have named you as my heir to the throne of England. If anything happens to me you are next in line. It is set in Parliament; you must protect the throne and the house of York, John, at all costs.

"That is why I cannot afford to risk the both of us being there and I owe it to your mother, my sister, Elizabeth Duchess of Suffolk, to keep you safe, she would not forgive me if I did not do so."

"But uncle—"

"No buts, Jack, this is what I have said and it will happen!"

"Uncle, we will not lose to the Tudor, will we?"

"No, John, we will not, God willing, but there are many underlying factors involved here, some of which you are not yet aware of. Please trust me and all will be well, I promise."

The waiting for word of the whereabouts of Tudor seemed endless, we filled in the time here by hunting for the main part in Bestwood because it provided close access to Nottingham should the messages come to us. And also it was good hunting, but again it reminded me of that day here, not that long ago, when Anne, my dear brave Anne, had headed off after the huge boar without a single thought for her own safety. I miss her now more than ever, I miss her love, I miss her sound advice, and I miss her not being next to me in bed at night.

Oh how different things may have been if Ned and Anne had lived to be here with me now. I have many good friends and yet I am lonely and alone. Pray Jesus that I can keep things together and do what is right for England.

We are now into July and still Stanley has not shown his face, I have instructed John to take the Stanley boy and keep him under close watch, in the event that Stanley does not commit. Our scouts are watching the port of Harfleur for any developments, and they are reporting a lot of activity. The consensus of opinion amongst the council is that Tudor will make for South Wales, to that end I have alerted William Herbert at Raglan Castle and Rhys ap Thomas, to muster as many men as possible and post look outs along the coast. One blessing is that if he does try to make for that coast he will not find it easy to land his army without detection.

At our council meeting last night, it was decided to send John Howard back to London, to oversee events there and when a more definite plan could be put into action he would rejoin us. John Scrope was dispatched to watch over the English Channel in the event that Tudor might try his luck at one of the Southern counties.

In the meantime we wait.

Richard and John were out hunting in Sherwood on a beautiful late July day,

The hounds had picked up a sent and were off baying loudly with the rest of the party after them. Richard pulled John back.

"Let them go, Johnny, I would talk to you."

"What is it, Father, is something troubling you?"

"Aye, lad, it is you that troubles me. But, Father, what have I done?"

"Johnny my son, you have nothing to reproach yourself for, you have always being my obedient and faithful son and I could not have hoped for better.

"You follow my instructions without question always, I feel for you, my son, because you are my son, yet in the eyes of the law you cannot be recognised as such. This does grieve me, as I would have dearly loved to bestow on you a title befitting a son of a King of England. Other than John Plantagenet, but my love for you is undiminished and always will be. And, as you know,

Anne loved you and treated you the same as she did Ned."

"Yes, my father, I have loved you all in my family, including the Queen, Kathryn, and I miss Ned very much. But most of all I love you, my father, because you have never shown me anything but love."

"Then enough of this banter, Johnny, what I want is for you to take some men at arms and return to my castle at Sheriff Hutton and look after my interests in that area there for me until all this is over. Take young Cecily and Bess with you. Will you do it for me, Jack?"

"I will most willingly, my King and father."

"Good lad, go and make the arrangements."

Chapter Eleven
Nottingham Castle
August 1485

I call my friends together for a council meeting this morning, "My Lords, I have not long received a message from Thomas Stanley to say that he cannot attend me here, as he is suffering from the sweating sickness, but will attend when he is able to ride again."

There is a jeer that explodes from all that are present.

"So that is that, Gentlemen, I think now he will not attend us and we are still in the situation of not knowing just which way he will jump. Also Northumberland still seeks to avoid me.

"As it is, I cannot hold out any hopes that William Stanley will lift a finger to help stop the Tudor if he comes up through Wales.

"So, Gentlemen, where exactly does this leave us? We may have Northumberland or not. The Stanleys may not commit and the best we may hope for is that they may just keep out of it altogether.

"At the moment Tudor may have something like three thousand men. But if he does land in Wales and is not stopped he could pick up another possible two thousand or so, we could be looking at in excess of a total of five thousand men, plus some cannon.

"Our forces at the moment are still looking a lot higher in number, but without Stanley and

Northumberland, we may struggle to match Tudor's total.

"On the positive side, we have a good number of cannon, archers, and men at arms.

"Also I have sent to York for as many of their good people as possible to come and support us.

"What think you, my good Lords? Can we beat this upstart?"

"Aye, sire we can, with one arm tied around our back."

"Thank you, Gentlemen, that is just what I wanted to hear from you, then let us make the most of our preparations."

The castle is alive with the sounds of busy preparations, blacksmiths shoeing, honing weapons and repairing amour. Sergeants at arms drilling their men and knocking them into shape. Archers at the butts. The smell of cooking on open fires, more and more men are arriving daily and we have had to accommodate some of them in the town, by the good will of the Mayor. The town's folk have been remarkable; bakers bring in baskets of bread, brewers bringing in barrels of ale, butchers with pork and women with apples.

I have sent to order of all our commissioners to review the soldiers they can muster and arm and equip them. Requisition horses all in the Kings service. All knights, squires and gentlemen to prepare themselves to be ready to serve. The penalty for failure is the loss of lands, goods and potentially their lives,

'Proclamation, The Kings will is that all existing quarrels be put aside. Henry Tudor and his supporters now in France, son of Edmund Tudor, son of Owen Tudor. He encrocheth and usurped upon him the name and title of royal estate of England, when it is well known that he had no right to this given, that he was descended of bastard blood on both his maternal and paternal sides.'

The proclamation warns that if Henry Tudor achieved his falsentent and purpose, every man's life, livelihood and lands would be in his hands. This would lead to the disinheriting and destruction of all the noble and worshipful blode of this realm forever. Every true Englishman should therefore resist for his own good.

'Richard has asked that his thanks be given to his subjects and knows that when the call comes, that they will as Englishmen, due their duty in service of the King. Signed, Rex Richard.'

We convene a further council meeting this morning and discuss all of our options and preparations, which are going well. The Mayor of London has promised to send to us a total of some three thousand men. And York are to send us men also.

Norfolk brings a thousand men.

We spend time while awaiting events, at Bestwood lodge and hunt most days, then on the 7th August comes the news we have been waiting for, the Tudor ships have been spotted, just off the coast of Milford Haven. They are making for a small port, called Mill Bay, near to the Dale. I feel almost relived now that we know where he is. So our instincts proved to be right, it is Wales after all.

I send messages to all my commissioners, but know that Tudor will have a rough march in front of him and will want to recruit as many as he can along the way.

Messages go out to Huntington at Raglan Castle and to Rhys ap Thomas, to move and intercept Tudor while they are still vulnerable and before they have chance to swell their ranks. It now remains to be seen which way Tudor's army will head for.

Back at the castle now, word seems to have spread quite quickly and you can feel an air of anticipation, whether it be in the town or in the castle. Riders come and go; there is activity in in the fields where crops are being gathered in as fast as possible. Johnny has left this morning for Sheriff Hutton, I will miss him very much, but he is a good lad and will do the right thing. Before he left we heard mass together in the chapel and the priest gave him a blessing, then we said our goodbyes.

I am alone now and only have my good friends to support me, since Kathryn's marriage to William Herbert I see little of her and have only the occasional message from her. She seems to be coping with her new life as Lady Huntington at Raglan Castle. I hope that I have made the right choice for her; she is a very caring young lady and will make Herbert a good wife. If they are as happy as Anne and I were, then they will not have any complaints.

Chapter Twelve
Nottingham Castle
August 1485

On the Move

0Last night was not a good one for me, as I tried in vain to sleep, it just would not come. In the early hours finally, I did manage to drift off into some sort of erratic nightmare sleep, where I saw myself trying to stave off foul evil forces that kept pushing me down into the ground. About dawn break I arose, went to the chapel and heard mass, it was still fairly early so broke my fast alone.

Kendall comes to me afterwards. "Your Grace, I bid you good day, I have news from our scouts in Wales. Tudor has moved his army on from the Dale and up trough Cardigan Bay into the Aberystwyth area. He now turns eastwards, my Lord."

"Ah he does try and make for Shrewsbury then. Bring me maps, John, and notify the council.'

At the meeting Francis asks if there is any sign that Huntington or Rhys ap Thomas has moved out to intercept Tudor.

"No there is not, Francis, and I have sent urgently to them, warning of the consequences if they do not. But

70

at Shrewsbury Tudor will be stopped, the gates will not open for him and then we may be able to pick him off where he stands. A further message has gone out to Sir William Stanley, instructing him to make all haste to Shrewsbury and take on the Tudor there. But it is perhaps my understanding that he may already be in Tudor's pocket. If he does pass at Shrewsbury, Gentlemen, then we must at all counts stop him well before he reaches London. If we look at the map, he has turned eastwards heading as we say to Shrewsbury, My guess is that then he will make for Stafford and Lichfield and try to reach Tamworth, then pick up the Watling street near Atherstone. His quickest route south to London. But we must not move as yet, until we know for sure of his commitments, Huntington and Rhys ap Thomas may well engage him and if they do, we move to back them. Do we agree, my Lords?"

"Aye, my Lord, we wait upon events to play out."

"We now hear that Tudor's army is at Mynydd Digoll or in English the Long Mountain, so he is just outside Welshpool. Our scouts say that the whole army is camped here, awaiting more supporters, which are arriving in large numbers. The hope that Rhys ap Thomas might engage Tudor is now dashed, as he has been seen arriving with very large numbers of men at this location in order to swell Tudors numbers. Also he is being supplied from all over North Wales now.

"There is no word from Huntington and I fear now for Kathryn, if he has turned his coat in this, then where does that leave her, pray Jesus protect her and keep her safe, as I cannot at this moment help her. But when this is over there will be a reckoning to be made.

"This afternoon I ask John Kendall to call all my Lords in full meeting of the council, Gentlemen you are aware of the events of the Tudors progress through Wales and of the treachery of Rhys ap Thomas and the Earl of Huntington. We now know that Tudor is making for to cross over at Shrewsbury, as we suspected that he would do. If Shrewsbury holds him, then we have to gather our forces to get there as fast as possible and if not then we still need to gather our forces to stop him elsewhere. To that end, Master Kendall I will now need you to send out messages to all of my commanders that are not with us here in Nottingham, at this time, to gather by the 16th of August, latest! John Howard is already on his way, it may be too late for John Scrope to get here by then, but tell him to do his best. Master Kendall, have the scouts estimate

The Tudors' numbers once they are on the march again."

"Yes my Grace."

"Thank you, my Lords; let us see to our men that they have what they need."

It is two days hence, the next we hear from our scouts is not good news.

Tudor has reached Shrewsbury and they have opened the gates and let him pass, he is now in England!

It is the morning of the 19th August, we leave Nottingham this day and head for Leicester. Mass has been said both here in the castle and in town, as we have a large force. Everywhere there are banners blowing in wind, the noise of horses' shoes on cobbled streets. The clang of steel and of armour. The Mayor and council have turned out to wish us well on our way; the town's folk have lined the streets as we pass through. Dogs bark, the men shout to the womenfolk. The cannons being pulled along, the archers marching out front of the line. The huge baggage and supply wagons bringing up the rear. We ride out in front, with trumpets blaring and drums beating.

These are my good people of Nottingham and they have done us proud, I will see to it that they have just rewards. This morning when briefing my commanders and captains I made it very clear to them to impress on all of my men that I would not tolerate any plundering of crops, or possessions, or any unruly behaviour whatsoever.

As we leave the outskirts of the town behind, I get to thinking of when Anne and I left here last to make our way to Middleham and little Ned's funeral. Such a lot has happened since then and I pray that they be with me as I prepare to do battle with the Tudor. Our progress is slow heading south, we have a large number of cannon with us and we cannot go too fast, we had hoped to be in Leicester by evening, but it looks like making camp for the night and entering Leicester in the morrow now.

I have received messages from John Howard and Henry Percy to say that they await my arrival at the White Boar Inn, I shall welcome a good night's sleep, as I have transported my bed with me.

The morning of the 20th August, we enter Leicester by the North gate and my retinue and I ride up to the White Boar inn, having dispersed the rest of my men in other parts of the town. Waiting to greet us at the Inn are

John Howard, his son the Earl of Surrey and Henry Percy. Howard grinning from ear to ear.

"Richard my Lord, I bid you welcome. We have news, my Lord; Tudor has left Lichfield and is now close to Tamworth making for Atherstone. We have him now, my Lord, he heads straight for Watling Street, it could not suit us better."

"Aye, John, it is fairly met indeed; we rest here tonight and move towards him on the morrow."

In the evening I call all my commanders together and we pour over maps of areas close to where Tudor must come if he takes the Watling street, which he must do with an army and cannon, if he intends to make for London.

We decide on an area which is known locally as Redemore and to make our camp on the higher ground of the village of Sutton Cheney. Thereby hopefully engaging the Tudor's army on Redemore Field. If he decides to make a run for it, we will have men placed along the Fenn Lanes to slow him up until we get there to engage him.

"So, Gentlemen, we move in the morning and make camp in Sutton Cheney. And may God be with us. Amen."

Chapter 13
Bosworth Field
August 1485

Treachery

The early morning of the 22nd August.

I have not slept well, being tormented by visions and by demons. No longer will I lay here in this restless coma. Arise that I must and make ready for the day is on us yet! The camp is eerily still, save for the guards that have been posted to keep watch. Some of the fires that were lit last night give off little wisps of smoke. The walk to Ambion Hill is not far from my tent. A mist rises up from Redemore field close to the Fenn lanes, some way off. I am not sure what it is that I was looking for, maybe the Tudor's men starting to make their way here. But it is still very early and I do not think that Tudor will make such an early march. It is over 10 miles from Merevale via Mancetter. If they are indeed making their way here. As I return to my tent, a shiver goes down my spine. There is a strange chill in the air. I rouse my herald and tell him to raise the retinue and break the fast.

Yesterday I moved my army from Leicester, where two days before I had my bed brought to the White Boar Inn, because the castle was no longer in use and was starting to go into disrepair (note, that I must see what can be done)

We are encamped at Sutton Cheney, which occupies most of this area, as my army is large. My spies confirmed to me that the Tudor was making his way to the south from Shrewsbury and heading towards Tamworth. The wretch is tiring to get down Watling Street and make for London! Good; I will Intercept him here and put an end to his treachery once and for all.

Before we turned in late last night, riders came to us with the news that the Tudor was encamped with his army at Merevale Abbey, just off to the west, near Atherstone. They also said that The Stanleys had been seen at Merevale Abbey. The Stanley's will have told the Tudor of our where a bouts, of that there can be no doubt. I do not trust the Stanleys in all of this, I have just received a message from Thomas Lord Stanley to say that Sir William and himself are camped at Stoke Golding and Dadlington and are awaiting our arrival.

Before I broke my fast I heard mass said at the Church of St. James in Sutton Cheney and on the way back, walked through my camp speaking to as many men as I could. They were in good spirits and laughed and joked as they made their preparations.

I write a message and have it sent back, releasing the Stanley son from my custody. It has served no purpose to hold the lad, he has done no ill to me and I see now that whatever transpires in the next few hours, the Stanleys will do what they have always done. And to count on their support I cannot. We hold a last meeting of all our commanders and determine that my Lord Norfolk (my dear friend John Howard Duke of Norfolk) will lead the Vanguard along with his son. With Henry Percy, Earl of Northumberland in reserve on the Ambion Hill. And if need will take the middle ground.

As for myself and my good standard bearer, Sir Percival Thirlwall, Lords Catesby and Lovell (my dear friend Frances) and the rest of my noble knights, we will hold and direct proceedings and when the opportunity presents, use our cavalry to scatter the Tudor's men, turning in on our right flank.

If perchance the Stanleys do commit, then they could bear down on Tudor from the left flank of Stoke Golding and Dadlington.

As to the extent of the rebel army, Tudor we believe has some 4000-5000 men. Mostly French, Welsh and some Scottish mercenaries. Although the Tudor is unproven in the field, he is commanded by John de Vere Earl of Oxford, maybe with his uncle Jasper Earl of Pembroke, and for sure, Sir John Cheyney. Sir William Brandon being Tudor's standard bearer.

If by chance the Tudor will not take battle and tries to make a run for London, I have mounted men stationed along the road in his path to stop him or at least slow him up and I will cut him down where he rides.

"What think you, gentlemen, is it a good enough plan we hatch here?"

"Aye, my Lord, it is a very good plan."

"Then let us be rid of this Welsh rebel usurper and settle him for good."

"Aye, my Lord."

"Make ready, my Lords and God be with us all."

After my friends have left my tent, I send for my armourer (my faithful and devoted man from Milan). Who has been with me now through many a conflict. My squire brings me my armour and he checks it most meticulously, then helps to fit it. It is such a good fit, I am most fortunate in having men such as these in my service.

At last I am ready, my tent is empty now. I pick up my book of Hours

And try to pray. My mind is on my dear wife, Anne, and my son Edward of Middleham, Prince of Wales, dear little Edward, both taken from me, these past months. Edward was quite often not well, although he was the bravest of little souls and in recent times seemed to be out growing some of his ills. I think of the happy times we all spent at Middleham Castle and at Sheriff Hutton. O that I were there now in my castle, out hunting with my beautiful Anne and watching young Edward being put through his paces as a squire at the Quentin. Or out riding across the dales with them both. What times we had and how I do love and miss them. "Lord Jesus Christ, keep them in your tender loving care and be with me this day in all that I do, Amen."

Finally I place my Battle Crown upon my helmet and emerge from my tent.

There goes up a huge cheer from my army, who are gathered all around and a cry of "Richard, Richard." My faithful steed, White Surrey is waiting there, we have been through such a lot together. As I mount him it is such a comfort, like being in the company of an old friend. I look out over the sea of faces that is my army, a strange feeling comes over me and I wonder if we shall meet again. My Lords ride up to me and beg me not to wear my Crown into battle, so as not to draw attention to myself.

But I answer, "I am the Anointed King of England, Richard III and will live or die as such, my men need to see that, as we ride out into battle this day."

Then I address my army, "Good men of England, we go forth into battle this day, to put down a would be usurper Henry Tudor and his band of rebels who for many years have sought to destroy the House of York, both under my dear brother King Edward IV and now your King Richard III. It is time to put an end to this, here and now, in this very place. Are you with me men?"

"Aye, My Lord we are!" went up as one

"Then let us take up our arms, God and St. George be with us this day."

The Cannons and artillery pieces have been moved into position and stand ready. The archers dig in their stakes and test their bows. Men at arms move into their positions. John Howard and his son are waiting in their positions I see Henry Percy with his men on Ambion Hill. We occupy the right flank, where the view is good, the mist from earlier on has lifted and it promises to be *a fair day. It is now mid-morning, Still no news from the Stanley's. Although we can see their men moving about at Stoke Golding and Dadlington, which is on our left flank. A message arrives from Thomas Lord Stanley. 'Richard we are in position and awaiting your move.'*

They may or may not commit, I cannot now decide or rely on them; we will have to watch them very closely to see which way they jump.

Riders come in, "Henry Tudor's army is in-between Fenny Drayton and here, my Lord, and they are making great haste."

"Have they Cannon with them?"

"Yes, my lord, we estimate a much bigger army than was first thought, no less than 5000 and may haps be more, my Lord."

"All to the good then, he intends to do battle and not to try and out run us. Inform the heralds to make ready."

All at once I have a great thirst upon me and dismount by a clean running spring, I lead White Surrey to drink and we both drink in our fill.

As I mount again I have this strange feeling, which I cannot describe.

It is not fear or anticipation that grips me, it is something more.

I see Tudor's army now, way down by the Fenn Lanes and the White moors. The heralds are there and I can see The Earl of Oxford's battle standard near the front of his army.

I can just about make out the Tudor standard which is way towards the rear.

At this moment, I see no sign of Jasper Tudor's banner, but no doubt he is there somewhere. I send to the Stanleys to move in from their positions.

A message returns, 'My Lord we will be ready to make our move once battle commences.' As I thought, the Stanleys are playing their game as they will usually do and may not commit. We will see.

The heralds return, "The Earl of Oxford will not yield his army and will not give or receive any quarter my

Lord."

"Very well then he has spoken, so let battle commence and God be with us all."

Just before midday I give the order to start the artillery bombardment.

Drums roll and horns blow, there is a terrific booming sound of cannon fire, as my artillery men open up. Flames lick out of cannon barrels and the air is filled with black acrid smoke. I have brought with me cannon from the Tower of London and also some from

Nottingham Castle, where we marched from to Leicester. Tudor also has cannon, but as we see not any amount. I see now that Henry Tudor has dismounted and is hiding amidst his bodyguard at the rear of the field and on one side.

The cannon on both sides pound away for very many minutes leaving wholesale devastation in their path, whenever the ammunition strikes home men and horses seem to just disappear from view. And then there is the awful cries of men that are wounded, some have been severally torn apart.

I signal for the archers to step forward and do their work; the sky is massed with arrow shafts in both directions, making that familiar whistling sound as they fly overhead. And the thwack as they strike home. There are already very many dead laying on the battlefield and very many more that are mortally wounded. The drums and horns sound out again and I see The Duke of Norfolk moves forward with his men, almost at the same time I see the Earl of Oxford and his vanguard move forward to counteract him. When they meet, Oxford moves his men into small units of wedge shapes and is therefore able to split Norfolk's line and to attack from both sides of the wedge shape.

Thus Oxford has now managed to break Norfolk's Vanguard and attack him from the rear as well as the front. After very intense and brave fighting the Duke of Norfolk goes down and is killed along with a lot of his men. Seeing this, my army regroups and manages to halt Oxford's progress from the centre. At this point I send a messenger to Henry Percy to come off Ambion Hill in reserve and reinforce the Centre and the left flank. He does not move his men! I send more messages to him to commit at once! He does not and just sits there! I send more messages to get the Stanleys to join the battle on the left flank, they do not!

Next I see out of the corner of my eye that Henry Tudor has mounted his horse and with his retinue is making his way over to where the Stanleys are (they still have not committed) The battle is not going well for me, I have lost The Duke of Norfolk my faithful John Howard, but also a large part of his command.

82

My army is fighting to hold its position, they will not be able to hold for very much longer I fear.

Northumberland refuses to move off his position and the Stanleys will not commit. My army is now very seriously outnumbered.

I see Tudor move back to his original position and again dismount his steed.

What sort of deal has he made with the Stanleys?

I now have to make a very decisive and important decision.

Lords of my retinue are called to me,

"My Gallant Lords and most noble knights, I beg you to hear me, it goes not well for us, with the Stanleys and Northumberland refusing to join battle, we are outnumbered and the men are tired. They will not hold the longer now.

I have made a decision based on these facts, we few mounted knights will make a last bid attempt to take down the Tudor, where he stands hiding in the middle of his bodyguard at the rear of the field, near to the Fenn Lanes.

It must be a swift action and one that I hope will take his commanders by surprise. If it works, My Lords, we may yet see the Stanleys commit for us.

If not, then we have done all that we can have done. Either way this day will go down as being one of extreme treachery. What say you, my Lords?"

"We are with you my King, even into the jaws of hell itself."

We have the squires bring our lances and make ready for the charge. I pat White Surrey affectionately, and whisper in his ear. "Dear friend and most noble beast, I have most need of you at this time, bear me well, let us ride like we have never ridden together before and God speed us."

Sir Percival Thirlwall moves up alongside of me, with my standard.

I give the word to make the charge and we move as one, trotting, canter, then into gallop. The horses armour clangs and rattles .We move as swiftly as a Goshawk, thundering hooves throwing up clods of grass. All around us the battle rages on.

As we skirt the main part of the battle, all at once it seems as if the fighting stops momentarily and men look on in amazement. I see Henry's standard ahead and make straight for it. "I will get him now, or die in the attempt." Up to this point, our charge has been such a surprise that we have encountered very little opposition. But now we are in Henry's territory.

We are eventually slowed and encounter fierce fighting. I see Sir John Cheyney coming at me from one side, there is clash and I manage to unhorse him. Sir Percival calls to me to look at our left flank.

All at once the Stanleys are making a move towards us, I recognise Sir William's standard. They are coming on fast, from in the direction of Stoke Golding "Finally they have committed for us."

My squire retrieves my lance, from where it fell in combat with Sir John Cheyney. Almost immediately he is cut down.

We are hemmed in, on almost all sides. I see an opening and shout to my Lords to follow, glancing back I hear a cry and see that Sir Percival has been unhorsed by a halberdier and is now totally cut off from us. He is *being attacked from every side, his legs have been severed, but he still holds high my standard. I have now reached a point where I am again able to see Henry Tudor still on foot and surrounded by his bodyguard, with Sir William Brandon bearing the Red Dragon Standard of Henry Tudor, mounted next to Henry.*

This is my chance; if I can now get to Henry Tudor it will be over.

I shout over the din of the fighting for my Lords, but can only see a few of them now. I tell White Surrey, "one last time old friend, one last time," and dig in my heels, He shoots forward and I see Sir William Brandon about 50 yards in front. With my lance raised high I go straight for him. There is a blow of my lance as it shatters in pieces, but no matter, as Sir William goes down and the Tudor standard with him. As I draw my sword, suddenly I make out the livery of the Stanley men.

A chill goes through me, a shout has gone up from them,

"A Tudor, a Tudor!"

Now I see that Tudor has mounted and is making towards his right flank, where the Stanley men are pouring in from. I move to try and cut him off. I am now within almost striking distance of him.

In my great hurry to get at Henry Tudor I have not noticed the bog, where White Surrey is now struggling.

All at once it seems that there are men on me from every direction,

I am unhorsed and find myself fighting men from all over. I manage to fell a number of them.

85

There is a shout from over on my left shoulder. I turn to see that just a few of my noble Lords have made it through the Melee. They have a spare steed in tow and desperately urge me to leave the battlefield now. I shake my head, "Nay, go and save yourselves, there may be other opportunities for you and for York, but I am the King and must stay and fight."

It suddenly seemed then as if the whole of the Tudor's army was upon me. I could hear that familiar soft accent that only the Welsh possess, with also a mixture of French as well.

It happened simultaneously, being cut down from all sides, I could not see, blood was pouring down my face and into my eyes. My helmet was being yanked off my head, I could feel my armour torn away, I was pushed forward.

Then pain, terrible pain, I, felt a something like a really Sharpe slice at the base of my skull, my head just seemed to explode! – Everything went black – Then nothing.

There is some debate as to who actually made the final killing of King Richard III at Bosworth Field or (Redemore Field) in 1485.

Some historians claim that it may have been Welsh mercenaries.

While others claim that it was Sir Rhys ap Thomas himself.

Sir Rhys ap Thomas was the other treacherous party in this battle, as King Richard had made him Principal Lieutenant in South Wales. He had instructions from Richard to stop Henry Tudor. But instead turned his coat and joined him on the 12th August.

Henry Tudor's camp just before the battle started, may have been at what is known as the White Moors, off the Fenn Lanes.

The remains of King Richard III were found in a council social services car park in Leicester, in August 2012, 527 years after being hastily buried, in what then was the Church of the Greyfriars.

On the 26th August 2015 King Richard III was reburied with great dignity and honour in Leicester Cathedral, being attended on the day, by thousands of people from all over the world.

Of the treachery that took place on Bosworth Field in 1485, only Sir Thomas Lord Stanley prospered and was made Earl of Derby.

Sir William Stanley: was accused of treason and beheaded in 1495.

The Earl of Northumberland, Henry Percy, was murdered, by a vengeful Yorkshire faction. Some four years after the battle of Bosworth, possibly by Sir John Egremont.

As for Henry Tudor himself: although reigning on the English throne for some 24 years, As Henry VII. His reign was not at all a happy one. Dominated by his mother, Margaret Beaufort, and always in fear of the many rebellions breaking out on a regular basis, he was in constant fear and always looking over his shoulder to see where the next threat would come from.

The 22nd August 1485 changed the course of not only English, but also world history.

King Richard III of England was the last English King to die in battle.

He was the last English King to make a heroic cavalry charge in battle.

He was the last of the most chivalrous knights.

He was the last of the Plantagenet Kings.

He was the last sovereign of the House of York.

He was a man who deemed Honour above all things.

He was a man of which we may never see his like again.

Endnotes

Richard III was born at Fotheringhay Castle Northamptonshire, on the 2nd of October 1452. To Richard 3rd Duke of York and Cecily Neville. As a child he would have been known as 'Richard of York'. In 1460 his Farther, The Duke of York and his brother Edmond Earl of Rutland were killed at Sandal Castle, Wakefield.

1461 his brother Edward wins the Battle of Towton and becomes Edward IV.

Richard is granted the Dukedom of Gloucester.

Richard spent some of his childhood under the protection and upbringing of Richard Neville Earl of Warwick (The Kingmaker) at his castle in Middleham, Wensleydale, North Yorkshire.

2nd October 1462, Richard Duke of Gloucester was appointed Governor of the North, Constable of Gloucester and Corfe Castles as well as already holding The Lordships of Richmond in Yorkshire and Pembroke in Wales. All of these would have made him one of the richest and most powerful nobles in the land.

17th October 1469 Richard is appointed Constable of England, following Edward IV return to power.

2nd October 1470 Richard and Edward flee to Flanders and seek protection of their sister Margaret

Duchess of Burgundy after Henry VI was restored to the throne by Richard Earl of Warwick.

April 14th 1471 The Battle of Barnett takes place, Richard is entrusted to spearhead the Vanguard. Richard Earl of Warwick is killed.

May 4th 1471 Richard takes part in the battle of Tewksbury.

18th May 1471 Edward set about expanding Richard's titles. As he neared the age of 21, Richard Duke of Gloucester is made Lord of the North, Commandeering Chief against the Scots and receives many of Richard Neville's titles and lands. He became High Sheriff of Cumberland, Great Chamberlin and Lord High Admiral of England.

12th July 1472 Richard Marries Anne Neville, the younger daughter of Richard Neville Earl of Warwick, in Westminster Abbey London. Through this marriage Richard was to assume the Earl of Warwick's power base in the North, including the Castle at Middleham and Sheriff Hutton.

December 1473 Edward of Middleham Prince of Wales is born, Richard and Anne's only child together.

1477 Richard and Anne join the largest and most prestigious Guild of Corpus Christi in the city of York. Richards mother Cecily had joined in 1455.

July 1482 Richard wins back Berwick on Tweed from the Scots, after more than twenty years, using troops from the York and Ainsty area.

April 9th 1483 Edward IV dies, Richard becomes Lord Protector to Edward V because of his minority.

June 13th 1483 Lord Hastings is executed at the Tower of London, for treason.

June 26th 1483 Richard Claims the throne because Edward's marriage to Elizabeth Woodville is declared illegal and therefore Edward V and Richard of York are also declared illegitimate, as are the other Children.

July 6th 1483 Richard is Crowned King at Westminster Abbey London.

October 1483 The Duke of Buckingham rebels and is executed.

April 9th. 1484 Edward of Middleham Prince of Wales dies, at Middleham Castle.

March 16th 1485 Anne Neville, Queen of England dies, of consumption (it may have been Tuberculosis) at Westminster.

August 7th. 1485 Henry Tudor lands in Mill Bay South Wales.

August 22nd. King Richard III is killed at the Battle of Bosworth, or Redemore Field.

The Tudor family came from Anglesey in North Wales, the basis of the Tudor dynasty was started by Ednyfed Fychan, who was a steward to Llewellyn the Great. Who rewarded him with lands in Anglesey and Caernarfon.

Henry Tudor was born in Pembroke Castle in South Wales, 28th January 1457.

He was brought up and raised in Pembroke and Raglan, by the Herbert Family, then, when the Earl died, by his uncle Jasper. At the time of the Battle of Bosworth he was twenty-eight years old and had spent a number of years in exile both in France and in Brittany.

Henry's father was Edmond Tudor, who married Margaret Beaufort, her second husband. His grandfather was Owen Tudor who was a courtier at Henry V's court.

He seduced Queen Catherine of Valois, who was Henry V's wife. And at some point after Henry V died it was claimed that they married. However there is no evidence that this happened. They had a son, Edmond. Edmond had a title, Earl of Richmond. But there is some doubt that Henry Tudor could inherit this title, although this is what he called himself, because his mother was Countess of Richmond.

Henry Tudor's Battle strength, in terms of men at the Battle of Bosworth, could have been much larger than has been first thought, as he picked up support once he landed in Wales. And although we do not know actual numbers and this does not take into account the Stanley committal towards the end of the battle. It is estimated by some researchers as being in the region of between five to six thousand men. Which may have been more than

Richard's army in the battle, given that Northumberland would not commit and the Stanley defection.

Henry had sent letters to potential supporters in England in which he laid claim to the throne, possibly around about November 1484 in which he states:

'I give you to understand that no Christian heart can be more full of joy and gladness than the heart of me, your poor exiled friend, who will, upon the instant of your sure advertising what power you will make ready and what captains and leaders you get to conduct, be prepared to pass over the sea with such force as my friends here are preparing for me. And if I have such good speed and success as I wish, according to your desire. I shall ever be forward to remember and wholly to requite this your great and moving loving kindness in my just quarrel.'

William Herbert Earl of Huntington made no attempt to stop Henry Tudor.

Neither did Rhys ap Thomas, in fact, it was Thomas who turned his coat and did the opposite. It goes without saying that Sir William Stanley could have made such a huge difference had he intervened to stop Henry Tudor in Wales, he did not.

Francis Lovell managed to get away afterwards with the backing of Richard's sister, Margaret Duchess of Burgundy, along with John de la Pole, Earl of Lincoln, Richard's nephew. Invaded England in 1487. They drew Battle with Henry Tudor at Stoke, Jack was killed, Francis disappeared and was never seen again.

John Scrope who had been sent south to watch the channel before the battle did not take part.

The men of York arrived too late to take part.

Sir William Catesby was captured after the battle. He was executed in Leicester three days later.

December 1487 Henry Tudor restored the Countess of Warwick's Beauchamp estates, but made her turn them over to him. She was allowed to keep the Manor of Erdington, where she lived until her death in 1492.

Cecily Neville, Duchess of York, died at her home at Berkhamsted Castle. 1495.

Margaret Duchess of Burgundy continued to fight the Yorkist cause.

Elizabeth's life with Henry Tudor was one of misery and tragedy, always ruled and governed by Henry's mother, Margaret Beaufort. She bore Tudor Seven Children, with three dying in early childhood and Arthur Prince of Wales dying at the age of fourteen. Bess died in 1503.

John Plantagenet (Johnny) was put to death in the Tower.

Kathryn Plantagenet, William Herbert's Wife, seems to have died, certainly before November 1487.

Edward Earl of Warwick, was imprisoned in the Tower from 1485-1499. Tudor then had him beheaded.

The What-Ifs of Treachery Against Richard III

Let us take a look at some of the "What Ifs" of treachery that took place during this period.

1. What if, after Margaret Beaufort's first backed and failed rebellion in support of her son Henry Tudor and continued passing of messages to him, Richard had executed her? Would this have put an end to Henry's invasion plans or merely delayed them.

2. What if, Rhys ap Thomas had not turned his coat and had pushed Henry Tudor back into the sea in Wales? We know that he certainly had a considerable amount of forces at his disposal.

3. What if, the gates of Shrewsbury had not been opened to the Tudor and had held him there until Richard's forces arrived?

4. 4, What if, the Stanleys had not turned their coats and had committed to Richard, either before the battle or during the battle?

5. What if, Henry Percy had committed to Richard during the battle and had come down off Ambion Hill to defeat Tudor?

It is fairly certain that if the huge amount of treachery had not taken place, Henry Tudor would not have prevailed against Richard. And indeed we may never have had a Tudor Dynasty at all.

We may still have been a Catholic country.
We perhaps may never had a war with Spain.
The English Civil War would not have happened.
The Irish problems would not have arisen.

The list is endless, we may all suppose what would have taken place "if" But this is history and destiny.

And has changed constantly over many hundreds of years, to become this is great nation we know today.

**Middleham Castle Leyburn N. Yorks.
Richard's beloved home.**

**Richard III and his queen, Anne Neville. Stained
glass window in Cardiff Castle.**

**Effigy and Tomb of Edward of Middleham, Church
of St. Helen and the Holy Cross Sheriff Hutton,
North Yorkshire.
The tomb is empty, but it is thought that
Edward may be buried in the Neville Chapel.**

Edward of Middleham, Prince of Wales.

Warwick Castle
Anne Neville was born here

**Fotheringhay Castle, Northamptonshire.
The York family home as it may have been in the
1400s.**

Scarborough Castle, North Yorkshire.

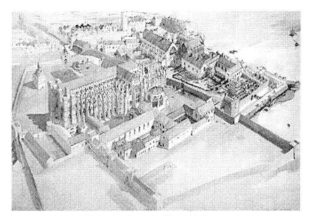

Westminster London.

Windsor Castle,
Anne Neville's preferred place to Westminster.

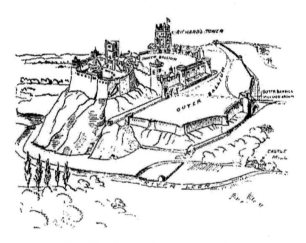

Nottingham Castle c. 1400s.

Epitaph for King Richard III from the City of York 1485.

The city of York inscribed into the city records for Tudor and all to see. For all to remember.

'It was showed by John Sponer that King Richard, late mercifully reigning upon us.

Was through great treason, piteously slain and murdered.

To the great heaviness of this city.'

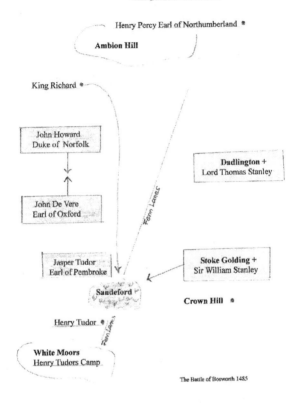

Sutton Cheyney +

King Richards Camp ✳

Henry Percy Earl of Northumberland ✳

Ambion Hill

King Richard ✳

John Howard
Duke of Norfolk

Dadlington +
Lord Thomas Stanley

John De Vere
Earl of Oxford

Fenn Lanes

Jasper Tudor
Earl of Pembroke

Stoke Golding +
Sir William Stanley

Sandeford

Crown Hill ✳

Henry Tudor ✳

Fenn Lanes

White Moors
Henry Tudors Camp

The Battle of Bosworth 1485

104